THE COSTUME COPYCAT

Maryann Macdonald

Pictures by
Anne Wilsdorf

Dial Books for Young Readers

DIAL BOOKS FOR YOUNG READERS · A division of Penguin Young Readers
Group · Published by The Penguin Group · Penguin Group (USA) Inc., 375 Hudson
Street, New York, NY 10014, U.S.A. · Penguin Group (Canada), 90 Eglinton Avenue
East, Suite 700, Toronto, Ontario, Canada M4P 2Y3 (a division of Pearson Penguin
Canada Inc.) · Penguin Books Ltd, 80 Strand, London WC2R 0RL, England · Penguin
Ireland, 25 St. Stephen's Green, Dublin 2, Ireland (a division of Penguin Books Ltd.)
Penguin Group (Australia), 250 Camberwell Road, Camberwell, Victoria 3124,
Australia (a division of Pearson Australia Group Pty Ltd) · Penguin Books India Pvt
Ltd, 11 Community Centre, Panchsheel Park, New Delhi - 110 017, India · Penguin
Group (NZ), Cnr Airborne and Rosedale Roads, Albany, Auckland 1310, New Zealand
(a division of Pearson New Zealand Ltd) · Penguin Books (South Africa) (Pty) Ltd, 24
Sturdee Avenue, Rosebank, Johannesburg 2196, South Africa · Penguin Books Ltd,
Registered Offices: 80 Strand, London WC2R 0RL, England · Text copyright © 2006
by Maryann Macdonald · Pictures copyright © 2006 by Anne Wilsdorf · All rights
reserved · The publisher does not have any control over and does not assume any
responsibility for author or third-party websites or their content. · Designed by Lily
Malcom · Text set in Breughel · Manufactured in Mexico · Library of Congress
Cataloging-in-Publication Data · Macdonald, Maryann. · The costume copycat / by
Maryann Macdonald ; pictures by Anne Wilsdorf. · p. cm. · Summary: Every year
Angela's older sister outshines her at Halloween, until one year Angela creates her
own special costume.
ISBN 0-8037-2929-4 · [1. Costume—Fiction. 2. Halloween—Fiction.
3. Sisters—Fiction.] · I. Wilsdorf, Anne, ill. II. Title. · PZ7.M1486Co 2006
[E]—dc22 2003026424

10 9 8 7 6 5 4

For little Leia with love
—M.M.

For Berivan
—A.W.

When Angela was four, she wanted to be a fairy for Halloween.

Her mama made her a pink tutu and wings.

Mama also made a rabbit suit for Angela's big sister, Bernadette.

On Halloween night, Mama made Angela wear a jacket.

"Fairies don't wear jackets," said Angela.

"That's because they don't have mothers," said Mama.

"You'll freeze in just a tutu."

"If I have to wear a jacket, then Bernadette does too,"
said Angela.

Bernadette put her jacket on under her rabbit suit,
and she looked adorable.

Everyone thought so.

"Oh, look at the cute little bunny!" said Mrs. Walker, their neighbor, who always gave out candy apples. She asked them to come inside so she could take their pictures.

She snapped two of Bernadette
and only one of Angela.

Angela tried to make Bernadette
vanish with her magic wand.
It did not work.

When Angela was five, she wanted to be a rabbit. But on Halloween night, it rained.

"I am *not* wearing a raincoat," said Angela. Bernadette didn't have to wear a raincoat because her witch hat and cape were plastic.

Mama sighed. "All right," she said, "you can carry my umbrella."

Angela felt proud carrying Mama's umbrella. But she couldn't see where she was going.

She tripped and fell into a puddle. Her fur got muddy and her tail tore off. She did not look adorable at all.

Of course, the mud didn't show on Bernadette's black cape. And the rain made her hair look more stringy and witchlike.

"Goodness, gracious me!" said Mrs. Walker. "You're just about the scariest witch I've ever seen! Come in here and show Albert." Albert was Mrs. Walker's cat.

Mrs. Walker asked Angela to wait outside. "You're a wonderful rat, but I'm afraid Albert doesn't like rodents," she said.

"I am not a rat!" said Angela. She didn't say thank you when Mrs. Walker gave her a candy apple.

When Angela was six, she wanted to wear the witch hat and cape. She practiced putting on makeup for days until she got her face just right. On Halloween night she looked so evil that she was almost afraid to look in the mirror.

"I like your black lips and green warts," Angela's father said. "You look really ugly."

But Bernadette looked beautiful. She was a gypsy. She wore Mama's gold earrings and silk scarf.

"You look just like a real gypsy," said Mrs. Walker. "Can you dance for us?" So Bernadette banged on her tambourine and turned around twice for Mrs. Walker and Albert. For that, she got a chocolate bar *and* a candy apple.

Angela cast a wicked spell on Mrs. Walker and Bernadette. Then she rode her broomstick home as fast as she could in the dark.

When Angela was seven, she wanted to wear the gypsy costume, but it didn't fit. She just didn't look like a gypsy.

She was tired of being a copycat anyway. So Angela decided to make her own costume.

She cut two holes in an old white sheet
and put it over her head.

She colored her eyes black with makeup. She looked
at herself in the mirror. She looked too plain.

Angela put on a straw hat with a big red flower. She rubbed pink rouge on her sheet cheeks, and she glued glitter around her eyeholes. She worked on her ghost costume until she looked just right.

When Bernadette saw her, she wanted to be a ghost too.

But when Halloween night came, Bernadette could not be a ghost after all. She had chicken pox. So Angela went trick-or-treating with Gerard Schwartz.

Gerard was a TV. He and Angela went to
all the houses in the neighborhood.
They saved Mrs. Walker's for last.

"Trick or treat!" they yelled.

Mrs. Walker opened the door. "Oh, my!"
she cried. "Albert, it's a ghost! A ghost and
a TV!" Albert yawned.

Angela shouted
"BOOOOOOOOOOOOO!"
as loudly as she could. She
jumped through the doorway so
quickly that Albert ran away.

Mrs. Walker did not run away.
She just laughed.

"You are the most *stylish* ghost
I have ever seen! I love your
costume," she said to Angela.

"I love your candy apples,"
Angela said.

"Have two, then," said
Mrs. Walker.

Gerard ate both of his candy
apples on the way home. But
Angela ate only one.

She saved the other to take home to Bernadette.